This book is a gift for:

From:

Date:

Trust in the LORD, and do good;
Dwell in the land, and feed on His faithfulness.

Psalm 37:3 (NKJV)

The Tasty Thumb

By Kelly Berry

Illustrated by Rachel Baines

The Tasty Thumb

Published by Clovercroft Publishing, Franklin, Tennessee

Published in association with Larry Carpenter of Christian Book Services LLC of Franklin, Tennessee

Illustrated by Rachel Bains

Edited by Christy Callahan, Dixie Phillips, and Rosanne Catalano

Cover and interior design by Suzanne Lawing

ISBN: 978-1-945507-71-7 (hardcover)
ISBN: 978-1-945507-81-6 (softcover)

Printed in the United States of America

Dear Parent,

Our childhood experiences can have such an imprint on our future ways of thinking. As children, our point of view is often beautifully filtered through our innocence and sense of wonder. As adults, we sometimes forget to marvel at the simple way children think about things they face in their own little world. This book gives an imaginary glimpse into the mind of a little girl who is asked to give up her thumb sucking.

Although *The Tasty Thumb* is a story about a little girl trying to give up her source of comfort, there's a deeper message to be found. It's what she does when she faces her problem...she talks with God. This is the Kingdom seed I pray will be planted in the hearts and minds of little ones when they read this book.

My time as a teacher and preschool director offered me many opportunities to observe little ones being comforted by their very own tasty thumbs. I would often ask those who were enjoying their thumb if it tasted like chocolate. This always seemed to bring a smile. Their reactions gave me the idea for this book. Thank you for sharing *The Tasty Thumb* with a special child in your life, thumb sucker or not!

Additional note: 100 percent of the net profits from the sale of *The Tasty Thumb* are donated to literacy projects and ministries.

God bless,
Kelly Berry

"But, Mama, I don't know if I can stop!" Kathryn exclaimed. She and her mama had just returned home after a visit to Kathryn's dentist.

"Kat, you heard Dr. Smiley. It's time for you to give your thumb a rest."

Kathryn frowned, blinking back tears.

Her mama stopped, gently lifting Kathryn's chin. "Sweetie, what's making you *so* sad?"

Kathyrn waved her thumb in the air. "I love my thumb soooo much. Don't you remember we would call it my tasty thumb when I was in preschool? We made up my tasty-thumb song because I couldn't remember all of my ABC's."

"Mama, we had so much fun! You would show me a letter, and we'd think of one of my favorite foods that started with that letter. Sometimes, I'd pretend my thumb tasted like those foods, and that helped me remember my ABC's."

"Kat, I understand why you love your thumb, but you're growing up. Don't you think it's time to give it a rest?"

Her mama gently gave Kathryn's thumb a kiss. "I've heard it takes twenty-one days to break a habit. We could get a calendar, and you could mark off each day you don't suck your thumb. How does that sound?"

Kathryn looked at her thumb. It did look kind of tired and wrinkly, but twenty-one days seemed like such a long time.

Touching Kathryn's shoulder, her mama shared, "When I have a problem, I always like to talk with God. Would you like to talk with Him about helping you to stop?"

Kathryn nodded.

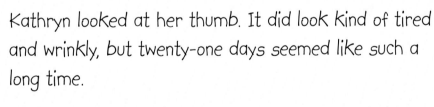

Kathryn slowly walked to her room and plopped down on her fluffy thinking chair. She gazed down at her tired-looking thumb, remembering what her mama said about giving it a rest. Then she curled up in her chair and closed her eyes.

Dear God, can You help me? I know I need to stop. Everybody wants me to stop—my mama, my daddy, and Dr. Smiley. My brother says my front teeth will start pokin' out if I don't stop. And this may sound crazy, but I think my dog, Sally, wants me to stop too. It seems like she barks sometimes when she sees me sucking my thumb at night when I go to bed. I don't think I can do this by myself, so I really need Your help. I love you. Amen.

> "I can do all things through Christ who gives me strength."
>
> *Philippians 4:13.*

When Kathryn opened her eyes, she stared right at her favorite verse that her mama painted on the wall when they moved in their house last year.

Kathryn thought about ways she could stop sucking her thumb. The craziest ideas ran through her mind. But, one thought made her jump right out of her chair, and she called for her mama to come quickly!

"Mama, I think God gave me an idea! What about putting a sock over my hand when I go to sleep at night? I'll call it my prayer sock—and I know just the sock I'll use."

Kathryn searched all through her drawer until she found it. She'd forgotten all about this special sock. Her mama tried to throw it out months ago when the matching one got lost, but Kathryn wouldn't let her.

She proudly held it up. "Remember? Nana gave me these funny socks when I turned three."

"Yes, I do remember, Kat. I love this idea."

When her parents came in that night to pray, Kathryn slipped her prayer sock right over her hand. Then she asked God to help her not suck her thumb.

The next morning, her mama let her mark the first day off the calendar. Kathryn let out a huge sigh. "Only twenty more days to go."

Days went by, and some were harder than others. Kathryn and her mama decided to make up a new song, *The Not-So-Tasty Thumb*. They thought of silly foods that would help make her thumb seem not so tasty.

An *A* might taste like anchovy applesauce, a *B* might taste like broccoli bubblegum, a *C* might taste like a caviar candy bar. . . .

Day after day, Kathryn continued to pray for God to help her stop.

Finally, Day Twenty-One arrived. Kathryn
looked at the calendar, and she got
a big surprise. Her mama had made
an appointment with Dr. Smiley. She
couldn't wait to tell him. Grinning ear to
ear, Kathryn looked down at her thumb.
She knew in her heart she'd kicked her
tasty-thumb habit!

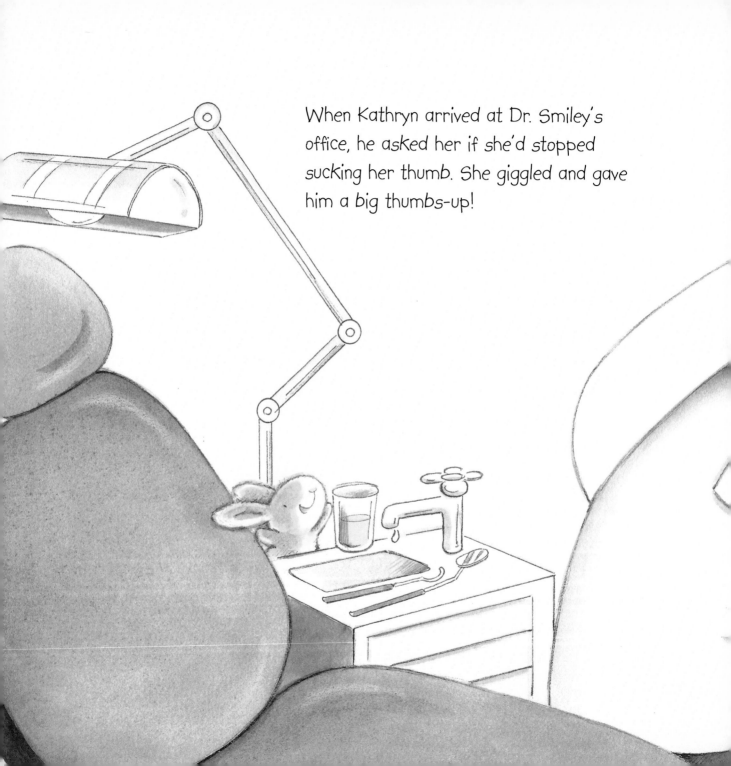

When Kathryn arrived at Dr. Smiley's office, he asked her if she'd stopped sucking her thumb. She giggled and gave him a big thumbs-up!

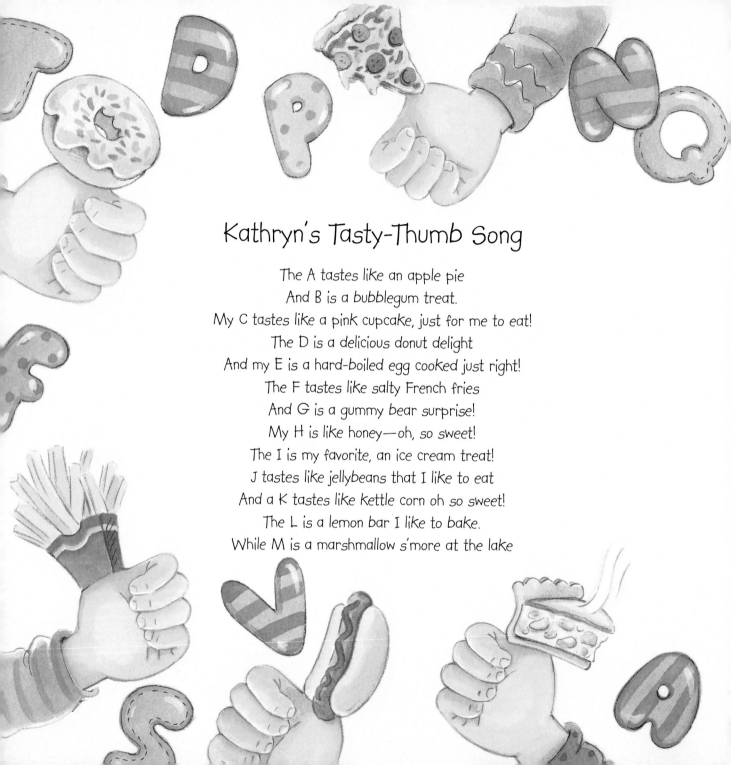

Kathryn's Tasty-Thumb Song

The A tastes like an apple pie
And B is a bubblegum treat.
My C tastes like a pink cupcake, just for me to eat!
The D is a delicious donut delight
And my E is a hard-boiled egg cooked just right!
The F tastes like salty French fries
And G is a gummy bear surprise!
My H is like honey—oh, so sweet!
The I is my favorite, an ice cream treat!
J tastes like jellybeans that I like to eat
And a K tastes like kettle corn oh so sweet!
The L is a lemon bar I like to bake.
While M is a marshmallow s'more at the lake

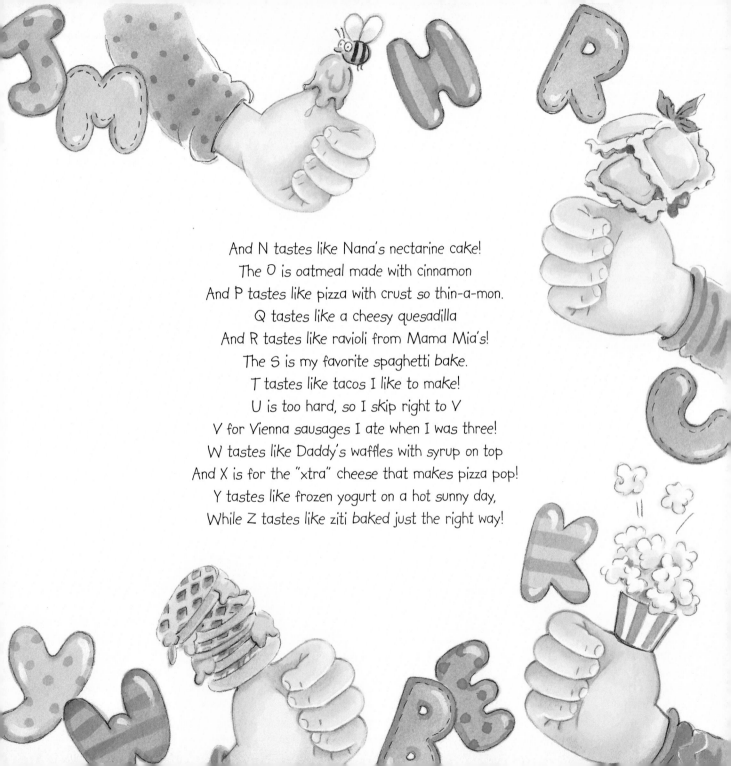

And N tastes like Nana's nectarine cake!
The O is oatmeal made with cinnamon
And P tastes like pizza with crust so thin-a-mon.
Q tastes like a cheesy quesadilla
And R tastes like ravioli from Mama Mia's!
The S is my favorite spaghetti bake.
T tastes like tacos I like to make!
U is too hard, so I skip right to V
V for Vienna sausages I ate when I was three!
W tastes like Daddy's waffles with syrup on top
And X is for the "xtra" cheese that makes pizza pop!
Y tastes like frozen yogurt on a hot sunny day,
While Z tastes like ziti baked just the right way!

Taste and See that the LORD is good!
How blessed is the person who trusts in him!

Psalm 34:8 (ISV)